A Christmas gift for

_____

from

_____

date

_____

THE CHRISTMAS JOURNEY

An original story by
SALLY FISHER

Illustrations by
DOUGLAS SARDO

VIKING

Dedicated to my husband
Norman Snyder
S. F.

Dedicated to my loving parents
Pete and Greta Sardo
D. S.

With special thanks to Barbara Katus

We are grateful for the late Loretta Hines Howard's gift to
The Metropolitan Museum of Art of its renowned
Neapolitan Christmas Crèche.

Many writers and artists—known and anonymous—have inspired us in the
making of this book. Among them is Christopher Smart, the eighteenth-
century English poet, whose Christmas hymn celebrates the kinship of all
creatures and the mystery of incarnation with incomparable directness:

> Spinks and ouzels sing sublimely,
> "We too have a Saviour born";
> Whiter blossoms burst untimely
> On the blest Mosaic Thorn.
>
> God all-bounteous, all-creative,
> Whom no ills from good dissuade
> Is incarnate, and a native
> Of the very world he made.

VIKING
Published by the Penguin Group
Penguin Books USA Inc., 375 Hudson Street, New York, New York 10014, U.S.A.
Penguin Books Ltd, 27 Wrights Lane, London W8 5TZ, England
Penguin Books Australia Ltd, Ringwood, Victoria, Australia
Penguin Books Canada Ltd, 10 Alcorn Avenue, Toronto, Ontario, Canada M4V 3B2
Penguin Books (N.Z.) Ltd, 182-190 Wairau Road, Auckland 10, New Zealand

Penguin Books Ltd, Registered Offices: Harmondsworth, Middlesex, England

First published in 1993 by Viking, a division of Penguin Books USA Inc.
1 3 5 7 9 10 8 6 4 2
Copyright © 1993 Blue Island Press
All rights reserved

A Blue Island Press Book
ISBN 0-670-85039-X
Designed by Douglas Sardo
Printed in Italy by Arnoldo Mondadori Editore, Verona
Typeset in the United States of America by Blue Island Press

CONTENTS

PREFACE

WHEN I WAS YOUNG I ALWAYS spent a few days at Christmastime with my grandmother in New York City. Grandma loved the city. Almost every day she found someplace interesting to go. To stay home all day in her apartment, she said, was a terrible waste of her senior citizen half-price bus pass.

I slept on her couch. Each morning we'd have breakfast in the living room and decide where to go that day. But there was never a year that we didn't go to The Metropolitan Museum of Art to see the Christmas tree. We would walk around the tree while the Christmas music played softly and look for our favorite angels, animals, and people. There were many others looking at the tree and the crèche—people of all ages from all over the world. Grandma always said that there were as many ways of looking at it as there were people looking, for each person there had a different idea of what the story of Christmas was and what it meant.

At night, back in her apartment, Grandma would tell me her very own story about the tree and its angels, and about the people and animals in the crèche at the bottom of the tree. The details changed a little each year, but this is the story as I remember it.

The Christmas story that I am going to tell begins at the beginning of the world. Way back then, when everything was new, the world was a better place than it is now. People didn't fight or hurt one another. They told the truth because there wasn't any reason to tell a lie. They lived in peace. Not only that; animals and humans could speak each other's language! It was called Paradise. And most wonderful of all, the God who had created Heaven and Earth still lived with us, and talked to people every day.

But somehow all of this was lost. Peace was lost, the friendship of all the creatures, and the familiarity between this world and Heaven—all were lost. Some people say that the great tree that grew out of the Earth and reached up into Heaven was cut down. Some say that humans broke the link by thinking they were more important than anything else. The stories differ, but on one thing they all agree: Paradise was gone.

Many centuries passed. Humans did what they could, and great things were invented and accomplished, though not all of these great things made us good. But even in the best and happiest of times, a strange discontent, a kind of loneliness, weighed on the hearts of men and women. They felt bereft. They wished to understand their lives. They feared that God had forgotten them.

Then, one winter, at the darkest time of year—when the days are short and cold and the nights are long and colder, and it's hard to believe that spring and summer will ever come again—on one of those nights, one of the longest and darkest and coldest, an extraordinary thing began to happen. A new star began to grow. Just like a brilliant flower in the sky, this star seemed to open its petals. It waxed large and white, and soon all those persons in the world who ask questions, the curious ones, began to wonder what this star was all about.

It happens that there were three kings living then, each in his far-flung kingdom, and each thought he was the only king on earth. You see, when you are a king, people do not tell you what they think. They tell you what they think you want to hear. That is why none of the merchants or other travelers who visited these kings ever told them that other kingdoms—and other kings—existed. Since the three kings had hardly been outside their castle walls, they knew little about life, but they all had one thing in common: They loved to gaze at stars. Perhaps they were hoping to regain Heaven. Whatever the reason, each one liked to climb his castle tower at night and stare and stare into the starry sky.

CHAPTER ONE
THE STAR

Jaspar was a handsome, tall, black man, the youngest of the three kings. His kingdom was in Africa. His castle was made of huge green stones like jewels, and only he, the king, could wear the royal color, green. Even his household pets were green, including his favorite, a turtle named Jade. Jaspar's mind was quick and changeable, now full of hope, then, suddenly, despair. One moment he thought himself a genius, the next a fool. This is because he was so young.

Jaspar wanted to be a man of action. He dreamed of great deeds and fine behavior. He longed for a chance to prove his valor and the purity of his heart. But he was afraid his great test might never come, or, if it did, that he might fail. He practiced riding and swordsmanship and kept himself strong and healthy and ready for anything. He was certain that he was meant, someday, to do something very brave and grand.

One winter night Jaspar finished dinner and left his great dining hall. The music and the laughter of his courtiers grew fainter as he climbed up his emerald-green tower to look at the sky and think about his future and his longed-for chance to do something heroic. To his surprise, he saw a new star on the horizon, much brighter than the others. Jaspar was stirred with wonder and excitement all at once. All he could think was that he must travel toward this star, which he felt sure was meant for him, meant to lead him to the great task for which he had been preparing.

Melchior was the oldest of the three kings. His kingdom lay beyond the Red Sea where almost everything was red. His red marble castle was filled with patterned rugs, mostly red, and even his gold was pink. Of the three kings he was by far the expert on the subject of stars. He was, in fact, an astronomer, self-taught, who had studied the movements of the sun, moon, and stars all of his life. He had filled books with his observations. His scientific studies so occupied him that he spent very little time in the company of others; he considered human beings something of a distraction. That is why most people, even those in his family, didn't feel very close to him. They were awed by him, partly. Often when he entered a room, everyone in it fell silent. Even his grandchildren were shy with him. They didn't call him Grandpa, but "Your Highness."

Late one winter night Melchior awakened feeling restless. He was tired, but not sleepy, so he slowly climbed up to his red battlements to look at all the old familiar stars. And then, to his great astonishment, he saw a star that he was absolutely sure he had never seen before. As he watched, he realized that it was growing brighter. That night, Melchior hardly took his eyes off the star, and by morning he realized that, for once, he could not solve this problem by himself. So he decided that, even though he was an old man, he would set out on a journey to find out if there was anyone in the world who could explain this star to him.

Balthasar ruled in the fabled blue kingdom of Godolia. He was neither young nor old but in the middle of his life. He was a very busy king. He was busy with everything; with his wife's new clothes and jewelry and which things looked best together, with his daughter and her new clothes and her singing lessons and her dancing lessons and her needlework lessons and her riding lessons and her elocution.

His family meant almost everything to him. After his family, he loved beautiful things: carved furniture, lavish embroidery, lace, patterned floors and ceilings, colored glass and sparkling silver, intricate miniatures, beautiful music, thoroughbred horses, fountains and gardens, sweetly scented perfumes, I could go on and on. He was always perfecting his palace, adding to his collections. He lavished most of this passion for beautiful things on his wife and daughter. Some nights he was so tired from buying new things for them, redecorating rooms for them, discussing new hairstyles for them that he could hardly go to sleep, there was so much on his mind.

On one of these nights, Balthasar climbed his shiny new lapis-blue stairs to look up into the soothing, starry sky. He was just beginning to think about how nice it would be to have one of his ceilings painted midnight blue with gold and silver dots, when he saw the brilliant new star. He watched it for a long time, and then a strange thing happened. Suddenly, impulsively, he said, "I must change my life!" He didn't know how, or in what way. He stood on

the tower, lost in thought, until he got cold, and finally he went to bed and fell asleep, filled with hope and confusion.

In the morning Balthasar awakened and remembered the star and the feeling he had had the night before, though he couldn't recapture the feeling completely. He decided to do the only thing he could think of to change his life. He decided to go on a trip.

Of course he wouldn't think of leaving home without the queen and the princess. They must all go together. You can imagine the busyness in Balthasar's blue castle as he supervised the construction of tents, folding tables, chairs, and beds, the choosing of outfits, the packing of trunks, the loading up of pack animals, the selecting and dressing of servants who would go along. It took a week just to get ready. Have you ever heard the expression, "All dressed up with no place to go?" That is what Balthasar had felt like all his life, until now. He was thrilled to think that finally the world was going to see him and his family in their splendid clothes and with their gorgeous entourage.

Princess Delphinia was the only child of Balthasar and Iris, the King and Queen of Godolia. She had always wished for a brother or sister because life was rather lonely for her. Perhaps that is why she loved animals so much. Whenever she wanted a new pet, her father would buy it for her. She had a blue-gray cat that she talked to all day long, and a blue-green parrot that she hoped would learn to talk to her.

More than anything, Delphinia wanted to be grown, so that she would know what to do in every situation and would never have to feel embarrassed. Then, she thought, she would have many friends and admirers, and would not be lonely anymore. Delphinia was very curious about the world, and so she was tremendously excited about the coming trip.

Iris had arranged for Delphinia's new traveling clothes to be laid out for trying on. When she saw them, Delphinia began to dance around the room. They were grown-up clothes—billowy blue pantaloons for riding, yellow leather boots, and jeweled earrings, the large dangling kind that she had been longing to wear since she was a little girl.

"Oh, mother! I'll look like a grown-up woman!" she said.

"For all we know you'll *be* a woman by the time this trip is over," said Iris. Iris was not looking forward to traveling at all. "You never know what will happen when you leave home," she said. "You can meet all kinds of strange and uncouth people, sleep in uncomfortable beds, and even find dirt in your food!"

Iris was worried about bandits and accidents too; she had heard terrible stories. And she was worried about her health. Iris always felt tired. She was afraid the trip would be much too great a strain for her. She had even tried to convince Balthasar to let her stay at home. "I'll be exhausted!" she said. "It makes my back ache to think of it! Do you really need me?" But Balthasar would not hear of it; his whole family must come along.

The day of departure came. Balthasar mounted his horse. The queen was helped up onto her seat on the back of an elephant. She carried a golden basket containing a supply of fresh, scented handkerchiefs, because she was afraid the elephant might have an unpleasant odor. Delphinia had a silver basket to carry, but she filled it with snacks for her new camel. When she climbed onto its back she was even more excited than her father, but she was very nervous too. She felt conspicuous. She was sure that everyone was staring at her. She wanted to ride her camel as if she'd done it all her life. She feared that she might look ridiculous. The truth is, she was as beautiful as any girl on earth.

CHAPTER TWO
THE JOURNEY

The royal family and its many attendants and servants rode down through the mountains and into the desert. There were days when they passed a few people going the other way, and days when the sun was the only other traveler. There were days so hot that they stayed in their tents and slept, and traveled at night by the light of the stars. The great new star seemed to move ahead of them, urging them to keep going, and telling them which way to go.

Finally, one hot, sunny morning, they saw hills in the distance, and soon they were among trees, with the desert far behind them. Delphinia spotted a mountain goat, and a pair of grouse. She was very excited. She had heard of these animals, but never seen them, except in picture books. At noon they entered a village on the edge of a great forest. Men and women, children and dogs filled the marketplace. Most of the villagers stopped to look at the splendidly dressed travelers and to admire them. But Balthasar and his family were just as interested in the villagers. Some were cooking and selling food, right in the street. Delphinia was fascinated. Iris was shocked. After much pleading Delphinia convinced her father to let her buy grapes, roasted chestnuts, and a hot sausage and eat them with her hands, something she had never done before. The sausage came with a large leaf that served as a plate and a napkin.

There were women of all ages in pretty embroidered dresses talking and laughing with one another. One fellow had a pet monkey, and another man, who looked like a magician, was walking two dogs so delicate and slender they might have been birds—except for their tails, four legs, and lack of wings. Pigs and donkeys walked the streets. There were men with homespun coats, leather bags and shoes, and thick wool socks with big cuffs. There were women who didn't wear any shoes at all. One man carried a pack on his back so enormous that Delphinia didn't know how he could stand up, let alone walk.

Men and women were busy washing fruits and vegetables in a running fountain. Nearby was a fellow playing a bagpipe and another with a mandolin. The music was louder and rougher than any Delphinia had heard at home, and she enjoyed it very much.

On the edge of town Delphinia noticed a small family, and a very sad-looking one. The little boy was crying; his mother was trying to cheer him up. His father was lying on a stretcher with bandages on his legs.

"What do you think might be wrong with him?" Delphinia asked her mother.

"I don't know," said Iris "It's terrible. I wish you hadn't had to see anything so upsetting. Try not to think about it."

But for many days to follow, Delphinia's thoughts would return to the unhappy scene.

That night as she was falling asleep in her tent, Delphinia overheard her father saying to her mother, "I must tell you, I am amazed to discover how enormous the world is, how many ways there are to look, to dress, to live! It makes me think that our blue castle in Godolia could be any color, any shape, and that we could wear any kind of clothes, eat any kind of food, and have our meals at any time of day. I don't quite know what I mean, but I mean more than I'm saying." Delphinia had never heard her father talk this way, but she had a feeling she knew what he meant.

The next morning, as Delphinia was riding quietly on her

swaying camel and gazing at the distant horizon, she noticed a long line of people and horses, like a parade, silhouetted against the pale sky. Just as she was about to mention it to her mother, she saw another group, very much like the first one, coming over another hill. She could see that these two processions, and her own, were going to meet where the roads converged ahead. As they came closer, she could see a splendid-looking man in a green cloak, wearing a crown, and riding a white horse, leading the first group, and an equally splendid, crowned gentleman in red, on a black horse, in the second.

Delphinia began to understand something that she hoped her father would be able to understand. These two men were kings, just like her father, Balthasar.

"Oh, this is going to be difficult," she said to herself. "This is going to be very embarrassing."

And it was. The roads came together. The three parties met with much ceremony; flags were lifted, trumpets were blown, and three small pages stepped forward to shout,

"His majesty, the King!" Silence. Each king dismounted and stepped forward.

"Good morning, I am the king," said Balthasar.

"Good day, I am the king," said Melchior.

"How do you do," said Jaspar. "Let me introduce myself. I am the king."

More silence. I will spare you the details. It took a long time for these three men, Balthasar, Jaspar, and Melchior, to come to an understanding. But, finally, they did. By then it was some time in the afternoon. And by then, I am happy to report, the three kings were friends. They had pledged their loyalty to one another and discovered that all three had left their comfortable kingdoms to follow the new, mysterious star.

That night the royal companions ate dinner together, comparing favorite foods, discussing astronomy, lifting their cups in toasts to one another. It was a great feast. All the cooks and grooms and other servants got acquainted and danced and sang until deep into the night.

During this wonderful banquet, Delphinia was seated between Melchior and Jaspar. She knew enough about proper manners to know that she should divide her attention equally between her two neighbors, but she couldn't resist talking mostly with Jaspar because he was closer to her age, and because he was so much more talkative than Melchior.

At first they discussed the difficulties of travel and the weather at home at this time of year, but as the dinner's many courses progressed the conversation moved on to more momentous matters. Jaspar wanted to know why Delphinia was following the star. She was surprised for a moment, then embarrassed, because the truth was that she hadn't thought about it. She was accompanying her father, who was following the star. She began to think that she ought to have her own reason, and that Jaspar must think her very childish for not having one. To avoid more embarrassment she turned the conversation back to him.

"Please tell me why you are following the star."

With this Jaspar himself became quiet and a bit awkward, but finally he said, "It is because I am looking for my great deed. I feel certain that my life will have meaning when I find the fine, brave thing I am meant to do."

Delphinia hardly knew what to say to this. She felt more childish and stupid than ever. After some flustered compliments like "Oh! How wonderful!" she became serious, and decided to speak as honestly with this new friend as he had done with her.

"I have hopes for my future too, but they seem trivial now that I have heard yours. I want to be grown up and know how to act and what to say in every situation, so that I will have many friends." Then she began to laugh, and managed to change the subject again.

As the days passed, the travelers covered many miles. And as the weeks passed, they became more and more weary with traveling and sleeping in tents. Most of their delicacies had run out and their food was becoming less and less interesting.

"Flat bread and beans again?" they would say.

One night after dinner Melchior noticed a vague light on the horizon. The next day they met two old women who were walking together along the road. The women said that the light must have come from Jerusalem, the great city of King Herod, where thousands of lamps burned at night.

The kings rode together all day discussing this interesting fact, and they finally decided something that seemed quite logical at the time: Since the world had more than one king in it, they reasoned, there must be a king more important than all other kings. If so, perhaps the purpose of their journey was to find this grand and powerful king. And if that were so, wouldn't it make sense that such a king could be found in the huge city of Jerusalem—namely, Herod? The towers of the city were coming into view. They decided to go there. Also, they were curious, and tired of beans and bread.

CHAPTER THREE
JERUSALEM

To tell the truth, going to Jerusalem was not such a good idea. The first thing our travelers did upon reaching the gate of the city was to ask where they could find the palace of Herod the King. The second thing they did was to get lost. The streets were narrow and winding. They couldn't see above the buildings or between them. They wandered in circles until the kings in front of the procession spotted the servants at the end of the procession walking in the street ahead of them. It grew late. Confounded and tired, they decided to spend the night at an inn and visit Herod in the morning.

The innkeeper took one look at them, bowed low, and said, "I have only two rooms fit for royalty. One has a big bed, and one has a very big bed. The rest of your company will have to sleep in the dormitory halls and the courtyard." It was decided that Delphinia and her mother would sleep in the big bed and the three kings would share the very big one.

Delphinia was not very tired, but it did feel good to be in a real bed again. "Isn't this exciting?" she asked her mother as they lay in the darkened room.

Iris sighed. "I'm glad you're enjoying yourself, dear, but really, I wish we could just go home now."

"Aren't you even curious about seeing King Herod?" Delphinia asked.

"When you get to be my age you are less and less curious," she said. "You just want to be safe at home where everything is familiar and you know what to expect."

Delphinia thought about this. She knew that her father was very curious at his age, and so was Melchior, who was even older. She began to realize that her mother was actually very frightened of

anything new. She felt great sympathy for her mother, who was falling asleep now, but, all the same, Delphinia vowed to herself that when she grew up she would try to be brave and stay curious. Finally, she fell asleep, to the sound of the three kings snoring in the next room.

The travelers rose before dawn the following morning to dress and prepare rich gifts in jewel-covered boxes to present to King Herod. The innkeeper himself guided them along the complicated route to the palace. Once inside they were led up an enormous marble stairway. Climbing it in their heavy robes was tiring even for Jaspar and Delphinia, but by the time Melchior reached the top he was breathless and dizzy. Finally they entered a grand hall and saw, at the far end of it, Herod's magnificent golden throne.

The room was crowded with subjects, most of them poor folk in tattered clothing. Delphinia thought that they must have come to ask for help, as sometimes happened in her father's kingdom, but, to her surprise, each subject held some small offering: a coin, a small bag of grain, an old piece of broken jewelry. Officials walked through the hall collecting these things, sometimes refusing the tribute that was offered, ordering the poor subject to return the next day with something of more value.

At last Herod entered. "I see that we have guests of some substance," he said. He was looking over the heads of the subjects toward the back of the room where the well-dressed royal visitors stood. "Clear the hall!" he shouted. At once the crowd left, barely making a noise. "Come forward, my friends," said Herod. "Tell me who you are and where you come from."

"I am Melchior, whose kingdom lies beside the Red Sea."

"I am Jaspar. My green kingdom is in Africa."

"And I am Balthasar, from the blue land of Godolia, and this is my wife, Iris, the Queen, and my daughter, Princess Delphinia."

"Welcome, my friends." Herod was smiling a weary sort of smile. "And why have you traveled all these miles to my glorious Jerusalem? Whatever made you decide to come here?"

"It was a star," Jaspar began. "All three of us saw it; a new, unknown star, that led us by some mysterious power to leave our homes."

Herod's expression was changing. A dark shadow seemed to fall across his face. Balthasar continued the story.

"We met on the road, brought together, I believe, by the same mysterious power that kindled the star."

"And now we are here," concluded Melchior, "because, in the course of our travels, we have come to believe that we were meant to seek out a king more important than any of the three of us, more important, even, than all three of us together!"

"How interesting," said Herod abruptly. "Then I should think your journey is over. You have found Jerusalem. You have seen me! My royal guides will show you the sights of this magnificent city. You will be given some gifts. You will then return home. Fine. Guides! Someone send for the guides! You will have a splendid day. You will enjoy yourselves. How nice to have met you. Goodbye." Herod waved his hand and looked toward the door.

"Excuse me," said Jaspar. "I am not sure, King Herod, that this is really what we came for." He turned to his friends and said quietly, "This doesn't seem right to me. Does it to you?" They agreed that it did not seem right and continued to converse among themselves.

"Very well!" shouted Herod. Then he lowered his voice. "Come forward. We will discuss this star."

What Herod revealed was that he too had seen the star, and that he had called for many advisors and wise men to interpret its meaning. They had told him that the star was a sign that a momentous birth would occur. A child would be born who would grow up to become a great leader. He would change the world. Herod said that he was very interested in this child, and that he wanted the three kings, if and when they found him, to come back to Jerusalem and tell him, so that he could go and honor the child himself. And then he added, "I will make it worth your while. I am a very wealthy king. You will receive rich payment for this favor."

When the travelers left the palace they walked the streets of Jerusalem for a long time without saying anything. Finally, Balthasar wondered out loud, "Didn't he know that we would have done the favor without payment?"

"Exactly," added Melchior. "It's insulting. It's very offensive. And worse than that . . ."

Suddenly Jaspar blurted out, "If we find the one we are looking for, and if he is a defenseless child, King Herod is the last person on earth I would tell about it!"

He had said exactly what was on the minds of the others. It was becoming clear to all of them that Herod intended not to honor the child, but to harm, and perhaps even to kill him.

When the royal companions returned to the inn they found their servants in a terrible state of alarm. Some were even weeping. "Robbers!" they cried. "They came in with swords and knives and threatened to kill us! And as we watched, they took everything of value. What a calamity!" The servants were all blaming themselves, walking back and forth, clapping their heads with their hands, standing up and sitting down, even rocking back and forth as if they had stomachaches.

"If only I had been here," cried Jaspar, "I could have fought them off!"

"No, no," Melchior said. "I think that would have been a foolish thing to do. There would have been a struggle and many of our servants might have been hurt or even killed."

Jaspar thought about this, and began to realize that it was true. It was probably fortunate that he had not been there after all, trying to be heroic.

Delphinia was watching her father. She thought how painful it must be for him to lose his precious things. But then Balthasar quieted everyone.

"Please, please! Let us be calm. And let us be grateful too. We are safe and sound, none of us is hurt." With this he hugged Delphinia and Iris—poor Iris, who was still trembling and saying, "I knew it, I knew something like this would happen."

It was actually not true that everything was gone, but almost. When the servants had calmed down, the kings began to look through their remaining belongings. In one bag Melchior found his golden box full of gold coins and medals. Balthasar was heard exclaiming, "Ha! My little jeweled chest full of frankincense! They missed that!" Jaspar uncovered his malachite jar filled with myrrh. And the tents were still there. And, of course, the beans and bread.

And so the three kings and the queen and the princess and their company left Jerusalem, planning never to return again. It was almost night by the time they found their way out of the city and left its high walls behind them. They were tired, cold, and hungry. Worse than that, for the first time since they had left home they were traveling back on roads they had already covered. It was clear that they didn't really know where they were going at all. The star was directly overhead, and did not seem to lead them anywhere.

How bewildered they felt, and discouraged. They could hardly remember why they had left home in the first place. The robbery was bad enough, but meeting King Herod had been the greatest disappointment any of them had ever experienced. It was frightening to realize that a great and powerful person could be so devious and cruel. They knew that he could do whatever he wanted to the people in his kingdom, and it was obvious that he cared nothing at all about their well-being. In fact, he would probably commit any terrible deed, if it would be to his own advantage.

The kings and the queen and the princess rode slowly along the road talking quietly about this, sighing now and then, until they were tired of finding new ways to say the same thing, and at last they fell silent.

All you could hear were the steady footfalls of the animals, a squeaking saddle, a dog barking far off on a hillside. "We'll have to stop soon and set up our tents," said Balthasar. His voice was full of weariness. The others heard him, but did not respond. "It's getting colder," he added.

They rode on, saying nothing, for a long time. Finally, Delphinia broke the silence. "Listen!" she whispered. They listened. "I think I hear music!"

"Might be a dog howling," said Melchior. They continued to ride silently.

"No. I hear a pipe playing. And singing. And I think I see a fire up on the hill ahead."

"Ah! I see it too!" said Jaspar. "It must be shepherds."

CHAPTER FOUR
THE SHEPHERDS

A shepherd, as you may know, lives a life as unlike a king's as it could possibly be. He lives outdoors most of the year. The hot sun warms him in the day. In the rain he gets wet. At night he builds a fire and sometimes plays a pipe to fill the quiet. He sleeps under the stars and is awakened by the light of the sun before it rises.

His whole life is sheep. He knows every single animal in his flock. He watches where they go, and helps them find fresh grass to eat. He is always counting them, because he mustn't lose even one. His clothes are worn and wrinkled, and they smell of smoke and earth and sheep—especially of sheep. When he needs entertainment, he sings a song about sheep. When he craves conversation, he gets together with other shepherds, and they talk about sheep.

"Hello!" Balthasar's voice called out of the darkness. "May we warm ourselves at your fire?"

The shepherds stood up to peer into the night, and began to kneel as the well-dressed royal visitors appeared in the firelight.

"No, no, please," said Balthasar. "We want no special homage. We are tired of the whole business of kings and subjects, and we are just plain tired as well. Your fire is so beautiful, we'd like to sit near it."

"On the ground?" the astonished shepherds asked.

"Yes. The ground looks more comfortable than a throne tonight. We would be very pleased to sit on the ground."

So, for the first time in their lives, Delphinia and her mother and the three kings sat down right on the ground. At first they didn't know what to do with their legs. They tried one position and another. Then, after noticing how the shepherds sat, they did the same, and made themselves comfortable. A silence followed.

The shepherds, you see, knew that it was rude to ask questions of travelers until they had been given something to eat and drink, but they were not at all sure that such wealthy and important people would want to eat their plain food. They certainly did not want to insult their royal visitors. Finally, one of the older shepherds spoke:

"We hope you will not mind, but all we can offer you is our usual fare: cheese, olives, fresh bread, wine, apples, and honey. We have no table, or even any plates. We hope you will understand . . ."

"A feast!" exclaimed Balthasar. "It will be an honor to share such delicacies with you." He wanted to ask whether they had enough for themselves and guests as well, but he was afraid the question might sound insulting to the shepherds.

There was plenty of food. It was a delicious, midnight picnic. When everyone had eaten, the kings told the shepherds the whole story of their journey, ending at last with the robbery.

"It wasn't the loss of our possessions that upset us so much," explained Balthasar. "It's just that, after seeing what Herod is really like, it made us feel that the world is not as good a place as we thought. You might say it was the last straw." The shepherds understood. They wished somehow they could cheer up their guests.

"*We* had a robbery not long ago," said one of them. "A cousin of ours took a little lamb and hid it—wait until you hear this—he hid it in a cradle, wrapped up in baby clothes! You should have seen it!" All the shepherds were laughing now, and they laughed so heartily, slapping their knees and throwing their heads back, that Delphinia and Jaspar began to laugh too. Soon all of them—including Melchior—were laughing so hard they could hardly stop. When they had finally quieted down, one of the shepherds began to chuckle, and before long everyone was laughing as hard as before.

Finally, they all grew tired. The shepherds made pillows out of their carrying bags. They fell asleep almost immediately. Without much thought or discussion, the royal travelers decided to do the same. Delphinia rolled up her silk shawl and rested her head on it. She listened to the crackling of the fire and stared at the thousands of stars until sleep came.

CHAPTER FIVE
TO BETHLEHEM

The dogs woke her. They woke everyone. They were barking and jumping about excitedly, and looking straight up into the dark sky. Did you know that dogs usually notice angels before they are visible to people? It's true. Animals are very sensitive to these things.

The dogs quieted suddenly. And then a whole choir of angels appeared, filling the sky with their singing, and shedding a beautiful soft light on the earth. The scent of spring rain and flowers seemed to flow from them. One of the angels spoke: "A child has been born who has been sent from Heaven to bring peace and goodwill into the world. This child can be found in the village of Bethlehem, in a poor, broken-down place in the ruins, lying in the straw, surrounded by animals." With that, all of the angels slowly disappeared, though the smell of spring lingered in the air.

Everyone rose up from the ground. They weren't a bit tired. Even Iris was ready to go to Bethlehem.

"Shall we dress specially for this visit?" the queen wondered. "Shouldn't we have gifts?"

"No. No." Balthasar answered. "We'll wear what we're wearing. We'll take what we have."

"How you have changed!" Iris exclaimed.

"Yes! And I imagine that I will change some more," said Balthasar. "I knew I must, but I didn't know whether I could, or how, or what to change into! I still don't know, really! But I knew I had to change my life. Now I know that I can. Suddenly our long journey seems worthwhile again."

They set off almost immediately, even though it was still dark. Bethlehem was not far, but traveling the narrow hillside road with a flock of sheep slowed them down. One of the shepherds, a man with a hooked nose and

dark, kind-looking eyes, seemed worried. He would run ahead of the group and count the sheep and then run behind and count the sheep. Suddenly, Jaspar, who had been watching all this, jumped from his horse and scrambled down the hillside. Very soon he reappeared with a tiny bleating lamb that had fallen to the rocky ledge below. When Jaspar had mounted his horse again, Delphinia said to him, "That was a great deed, worthy of a hero!"

"Oh, no," he answered. "Not really."

"*He* thinks it was a great deed," she said, nodding toward the shepherd, who was walking along petting the lamb, which he had tucked into his shoulder bag. "And so do I."

The sky in the east was white and gold, though the sun had not yet risen. Delphinia had the strange impression that she was able to see everything much more clearly than usual. As they passed through trees, it seemed to her that every single leaf was distinctly visible. She noticed a rabbit in the grass, perfectly still, looking right at her. Then she saw an owl in a tree, watching the travelers. The more closely she looked the more animals she noticed: doves, foxes, hawks, bears, mice, lizards, even spinks and ouzels (birds so shy that they are almost unheard of). Most astonishing of all, a beautiful stag wearing his crown of antlers was walking behind the trees, keeping pace with the travelers going toward Bethlehem.

The sun was rising as they reached their destination. It was such a small town—just an inn and a few houses really—that they had no trouble finding the place that the angel had described. There, beneath the ruins of an ancient building, was a family of three; a man, a woman, and a newborn baby. The mother had made a baby's bed out of a wooden feed trough lined with straw and pieces of cloth. The baby was sound asleep. The family seemed to glow with pleasure and peacefulness.

CHAPTER SIX
THE BABY

Have you ever seen a newborn child? It is smaller than you think. Its eyes are as dark as the night sky. What do they see? Its tiny hands have not held a thing on earth. What will they hold? Its small, soft feet have never been walked upon. Where will they go?

Melchior was the first to approach the manger and behold the baby. He removed his crown. He placed his box of gold in the straw. The baby's eyes opened, and Melchior looked deeply into them.

"From the night I first saw the new star," he said to himself, "I began to realize that I have been mistaken all of my life. I have tried to live apart from others. I thought the world was full of evil, while the starry sky was perfect. I thought my studies would suffer if I shared my thoughts with anyone. Since then I have met people who can teach me so much, about the world, and even about the stars. And look at this infant; it will not even learn to walk without the help of adults! Human beings must help one another if they are to accomplish anything. How I wish I had understood this earlier. I will go home and get to know my grandchildren better. I will teach them what I can. Perhaps one will want to become an astronomer!" Melchior's thoughts raced on until finally they went too fast even for him. He smiled an enormous smile and picked up the baby's little foot between his thumb and fingers and gave it a kiss.

Jaspar walked up next, his crown in one hand and in the other the malachite jar of myrrh. He placed it next to the box of gold. Jaspar had never seen a newborn baby before. It almost frightened him to see how tiny and fragile he was. In some way the child reminded him of the soft, bony little lamb he had held that very morning. And that is when Jaspar realized that his opportunity to do some great deed might never come. He understood that perhaps he had wanted to be heroic just for himself. A whole life of small kindnesses would be a very great thing, he realized, even if it would never

make him famous. All of this came to him in just one moment's time, and it made him very happy. In some secret way he couldn't explain, he knew his life made sense. He touched the baby's head and felt the little soft place in the middle of it and closed his eyes.

Then Balthasar gave his crown to Iris to hold, and walked up to see the little family. He did not take his eyes off them as he bent down to place the jewel-covered chest of frankincense in the straw. The woman, the man, and the child, all three looked so beautiful that they seemed to glow from within.

"I have always sought beauty," Balthasar thought to himself. "I have always tried to capture it, to buy it, to own it. But the beauty of this scene can only be beheld, and then remembered. I can't pack it up and take it home." He stood silent for a while. "And their beauty has nothing to do with riches. They would not be more beautiful with all of my finery and jewels, or even Herod's. I have been so busy, so preoccupied with getting and fixing and buying and building that I have not felt at all the sweetness of the beauty of my life. I have so much to learn. What an amazing adventure is ahead of me. I will never be busy again!" As usual, Balthasar meant more than he was able to put in words. He kissed the baby on the cheek and breathed in its sweet, human smell.

As Iris walked up to the manger she was reminded of another family of three. She was reminded of a young mother, a crying little boy, and a father with bandaged legs.

"Why am I thinking of them now?" she asked herself. And the answer came to her: "It's because I have been trying not to, ever since I saw them. I wonder what was wrong with the man? Was it a war wound? Was it a disease?" For the first time, she was not afraid to imagine their lives.

"Perhaps I will see them again on the way home," she thought. "Perhaps there's something I can do to help." Iris didn't realize then that she was becoming a new person. She didn't know that she had stopped worrying about all the bad things that might happen to her. She didn't even notice that she wasn't tired. She looked at the infant and lifted its tiny hand with her fingers. "What a lovely child!" she said to herself. "And look how comfortable he is in an animal's manger. I never would have thought one could make a bed of such a thing. What a clever mother!" She could see how poor the family was. She hoped the gifts would be of some use to them. "I wonder what they'll do with gold and frankincense and myrrh," she thought. Iris was filled with curiosity. As she walked back to the others she was thinking: "I'm so glad I made this journey. Whatever was it that made me want to stay at home?"

When Delphinia approached the manger she couldn't help noticing the ox and the donkey that were standing behind it. They made the infant look even tinier than it was. Just then two shepherds appeared, and as they bent toward the child they put their arms over the animals' shoulders and leaned on them.

"Like old friends," she thought. It was then that something extraordinary happened to Delphinia, something she was never able to explain or describe, though she remembered it for the rest of her life. "We are all old friends," she said to herself. She was looking at the faces around her, the baby's, the woman's, the man's, the shepherds', the ox's face, the donkey's, and she saw something in all their eyes—even in their noses and mouths, their ears and necks and shoulders—something so familiar that she said, "All of us are brothers and sisters. We are one family." And she felt a feeling that can only be described as the absolute opposite of loneliness. "I will remember this," she thought. "I don't have to worry about saying the right thing and doing the right thing and having enough friends. I simply have to remember that we are all one family, human beings, and even animals."

The infant began to squirm and whimper. The mother lifted him to her breast to feed. "Just like a baby lamb," thought Delphinia. She touched the baby's little shoulder. As she turned to rejoin her family and friends she saw the magnificent stag with his crown of antlers, standing at the edge of the forest like a fourth king, an emissary from the kingdom of the animals.

Important events are often invisible. The people who left Bethlehem that morning looked just like the people who had come. But within each of them a change had taken place, a change in how he or she saw the world. So, for each of them, the world itself had changed. Sometimes a journey will do this; sometimes a baby will do this; and sometimes it is a completely mysterious force that does this. When it happens, life begins anew.

The royal companions decided to begin their journey home. They said goodbye to the shepherds. Before they left, Jaspar warned the little family that King Herod was a great threat to them. They thanked him and said that they would travel out of his reach.

Melchior, Jaspar, Balthasar, Iris, and Delphinia had many long conversations in the days that followed. As they traveled they talked about what had happened to each of them in Bethlehem, and they continued to discover more about themselves and each other. They parted at the spot where the road branched out, promising always to be friends, and to visit one another often.

EPILOGUE

THAT IS MY GRANDMOTHER'S STORY. But when she finished, she would say:

"Do you remember the great forest in the middle of the crèche? Remember how, when you look up, you see that it is really the bottom of an enormous tree? That tree is the link between Heaven and Earth, the one I told you about at the very beginning of the story. Its roots sink down into the deep unknown, and its branches reach into the stars and through a wide door in the dark sky. It is like a staircase for the messengers of Heaven. Angels ascend the earthy-smelling pine branches to enter the world above, angels also descend from branch to branch to the world below. The vessels they hold are filled with incense—perhaps it's frankincense or myrrh—to give us a taste of the fragrance of Paradise. The tree is an evergreen, to remind us in the winter that the green leaves of spring will come again. It is the giant undying tree that holds the universe together. It is the center of the world.

The Christmas tree and crèche at The Metropolitan Museum of Art combine two Christmas traditions. Loretta Hines Howard, who gave the beautiful figures to the Museum, first put these two traditions together by placing a manger scene at the bottom of the Christmas tree and hanging the angels—which would usually be suspended in the sky above the manger—on the tree.

The figures in the Museum's crèche come from Naples, Italy, and were made in the eighteenth century. They represent the animals, shepherds, and peasants of southern Italy at that time, as well as many Asians and others from faraway places who join in the universal homage given to the infant Jesus. Except for the Holy Family, none of the figures is dressed in attire appropriate to the actual time of Christ, because the birth of the Christ child was seen to be a living, contemporary event as well as an historical one.

Most of the figures have faces made of painted terra-cotta (the red clay that flowerpots are made of) and painted wooden arms, hands, and feet. Their bodies are flax or hemp reinforced with wire. Their clothing is made of silk and other fabrics, sewn by hand, and finished in wonderful detail.

Crèches, or manger scenes, are commonly used in homes and churches in the countries of central and southern Europe. If you were to travel through Spain, for example, at Christmastime, you would see booths set up in town and city squares where you could buy figures of the Holy Family, the three kings, shepherds, and animals, as well as miniature trees and bushes. Some booths would offer large pieces of bark and moss, and even rocks, for use in crèche backgrounds.

Christmas trees are traditional in northern Europe. They go back much earlier than Christianity and were probably used on the midwinter holidays thousands of years ago. Their symbolism is easy to understand. When most trees are bare and it looks as if nothing will ever grow again, the evergreen tree reminds us that the world is not really dead. When it is decorated, it looks like a fruit tree in summer, bearing fruit. Candles and lights are important for the midwinter holidays too. They are used near the winter solstice when the nights are longest and the days shortest. In very early societies, they may have been thought to dispel the darkness and make the sun reverse its pattern.

The ancient idea of the tree of life is found all over the world, among people of many different cultures and religions. This is the great tree that has its roots in the underworld and its topmost branches in Heaven.